This book belongs to
my friend:

A NOTE TO PARENTS

People respond to music from a very early age. Children love to bounce, sway, and jump to lively tunes, and they create their own compositions by making a variety of noises using household items and/or their feet, hands, and voices. In *Oswald Makes Music*, Oswald and his friends discover that they do not need expensive instruments to create a unique symphony of sound.

Reading *Oswald Makes Music* aloud with your child offers a special opportunity to be silly together making your own music by repeating the sounds in the story. Take turns creaking, zipping, and whomping. Assign different noises to different family members for the full orchestral effect. In addition, encourage your child to create new sounds for the characters.

Continue experiencing the joy of music long after the book is closed. Notice and talk about everyday sounds—the doorbell, running water, and feet on the stairs. Listen to all types of music together, and make musical instruments out of objects you have around the house—a wooden spoon on a bowl or beans inside two paper cups taped together. Be creative! Seek out sing-along programs and child-friendly concerts, often hosted by libraries, museums, and community centers.

Learning Fundamental: 🎺 **music + movement**

For more parent and kid-friendly activities, go to www.nickjr.com.

Published by Scholastic Inc., 90 Old Sherman Turnpike, Danbury, CT 06816

SCHOLASTIC and associated logos are trademarks and/or registered trademarks of Scholastic Inc.

ISBN 0-7172-6622-2

Printed in the U.S.A.

First Scholastic Printing, October 2002

OSWALD MAKES MUSIC

by
Dan Yaccarino

illustrated by
Tom Mangano

SCHOLASTIC INC.

New York   Toronto   London   Auckland   Sydney
Mexico City   New Delhi   Hong Kong   Buenos Aires

Oswald the octopus and his pet hot dog, Weenie, were enjoying a quiet afternoon in Big City Park. Suddenly they heard the most wonderful music. Where was it coming from?

Why, there it was!

"Gosh, Weenie," said Oswald, "that sure is great music!" Oswald couldn't help but sway back and forth.

Weenie wagged her tail. A bird and a squirrel stopped by to listen.

TAPPITY
TAP
TAP!

"Gee, Weenie," said Oswald, "wouldn't it
be swell if we could make music like that?"
Weenie wagged her tail some more.
Oswald picked up a stick and tapped it.
"TAPPITY TAP TAP!"

"**SWISH! SWISH!**" went Weenie's tail.
"**CHEEP! CHEEP!**" chirped the bird.
"**CLICK CLICKY!**" clicked the squirrel.

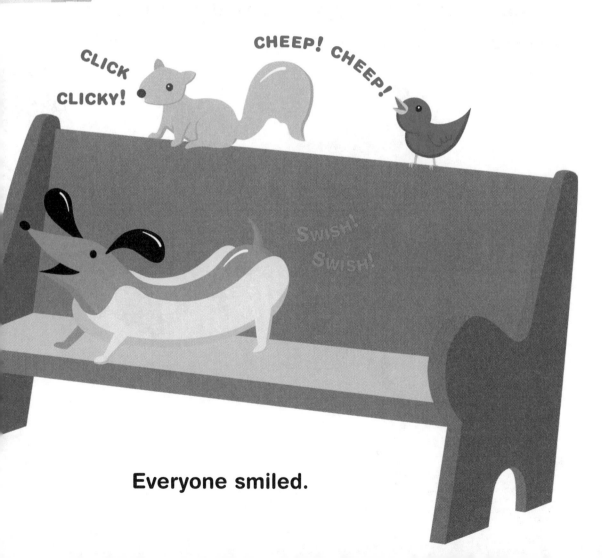

CLICK
CLICKY!

CHEEP! CHEEP!

SWISH!
SWISH!

Everyone smiled.

"Hey there, Oswald!" shouted Daisy as she roller-skated up to them.

"Hi, Daisy," Oswald said. "Did you hear that beautiful music? We don't have real instruments, but we're making our own sounds. Do you want to join us?"

ZIP!

ZIP! ZIP!

"I doodley-do!" exclaimed Daisy.
"**ZIP! ZIP! ZIP!**" went Daisy's roller skates.

Everyone giggled.

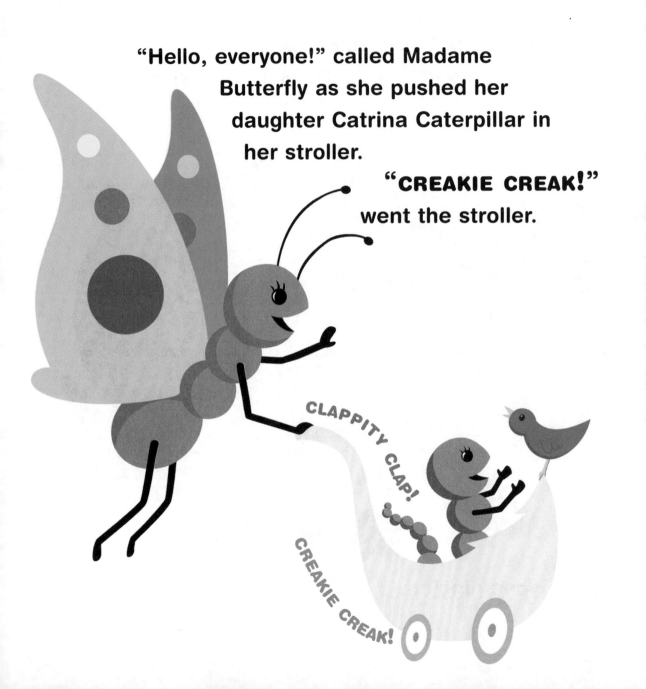

"Hello, everyone!" called Madame Butterfly as she pushed her daughter Catrina Caterpillar in her stroller.

"**CREAKIE CREAK!**" went the stroller.

CLAPPITY CLAP!

CREAKIE CREAK!

Catrina happily clapped when she saw Oswald.
"CLAPPITY CLAP!" went Catrina.

Everyone beamed.

The Egg Twins, Egbert and his brother, Leo, happened by on their way to play a bit of badminton.

"Greetings all!" said Egbert. "What a lovely day!"

"Yes! Yes!" said Leo. "And what lovely music!"

"Why, thank you," Oswald said.
"Is there a sound you'd like to make?"
The Egg Twins smiled, and Leo
bounced the badminton birdie on his
racquet.

"**BOING! BOING!**" went the birdie.

Everyone chuckled.

"Say, what's all the hubbub?" cried Henry. "I'm trying to read my newspaper!"

"We're having a swell time making our own music," Oswald told him.

"But you can only make music with real instruments," said Henry.

Oswald rolled up Henry's newspaper and gave it back to him. "Blow into it," Oswald encouraged. "**TOOT! TOOOT!**" went Henry.

Everyone grinned.

"Weee doggies!" shouted Cactus Pete.
"That sure is perty music!" said Cactus Polly.

They wanted to get in on the fun as well!
"**WHOMP! WHOMP!**" went their ropes.

Everyone hooted.

Steve Tree walked up with Woodrow, his pet woodpecker.

"Hello, all," said Steve. "Where is that gorgeous music coming from?"

"From us," Oswald explained. "We're making the music!"

RAPPITY RAP RAP!

"Can we play, too?" Steve asked.
"Of course," everyone replied.
"**RAPPITY RAP RAP!**" buzzed
Woodrow.

Everyone laughed.

"My word! That is lovely music!" said Johnny Snowman.

"Thank you," Oswald said.

"We're making music without any instruments at all!
Why don't you join us?" Oswald asked.
"**TOOO-WEE!**" Johnny Snowman whistled.
Everyone applauded.

SQUEAKIE!
SQUEAKIE!

Suddenly they all heard a very strange sound.
Who made that noise? No one knew. There it
was again.

Why, it was Andy the Candy Pumpkin! He had
been listening to the music from behind a tree.
The strange sound was his very squeaky shoes.
   "SQUEAKIE! SQUEAKIE!" his shoes squealed.

Everyone howled.

KA-CHOO!

"Hi, everybody!" called Pongo the friendly dragon.
"What are you up to, Pongo?" asked Oswald.
"I've been smelling the beautiful flowers in the park, but they make me sneeze," Pongo explained.

"Why, that'll be perfect for our band!" Oswald told him.
"How?" Pongo asked. "All I do is . . . **KA-CHOO!**"

Everyone said, "*Gesundheit!*"

Friends from everywhere gathered around the musicians. "*Bravo! Bravo!*" they all exclaimed. "That was beautiful music, but where are your instruments?"

"Well, we don't have drums or tubas or clarinets," Oswald explained, "but we found another way to make music."

"Wow! You're as good as our band," one of the tin soldiers said. "It's too bad you don't have a leader."

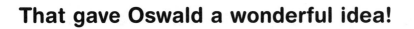

That gave Oswald a wonderful idea!